SAM PATCH

THE BIG TIME JUMPER

by
Carol Beach York

illustrated by
Bert Dodson

Folk Tales of America

Troll Associates

PROLOGUE

Sam Patch was born in Reading, Massachusetts, on June 17, 1799, but he lived a large part of his life in New Jersey. Sam became famous as a daredevil jumper and drew great crowds wherever he jumped.

Although there were no radios or television sets back in Sam's day, the newspapers carried notices of his jumps. When he jumped from Niagara Falls, the Buffalo *Republican* wrote:

The jump of Patch is the greatest feat ever made by a person. He may now challenge the universe for a competitor.

Niagara Falls wasn't Sam's first jump. And it wasn't his last. His life was always full of excitement, and it is possible that the stories have become just a little exaggerated through the years. This story is about what happened before Niagara Falls. And about what happened afterward.

Library of Congress # 79-66318
ISBN 0-89375-306-8/0-89375-305-X (pb)

Sam Patch was born to jump.

He was born in 1799, so his first jump was into a whole new century!

The next jump he made was out of his mother's arms into a washtub of soapsuds. He landed with a grand splash. Soapy water flew everywhere.

"Look at this!" Mrs. Patch exclaimed. She wiped soap bubbles from her chin. "Did you ever see such a child?"

Mr. Patch was eating his breakfast. He was far enough across the room, so he didn't get splattered by the water. Safe and dry, he said calmly, "Jumping's all right for a baby. He'll settle down soon enough."

But Sam didn't settle down. Pretty soon he was jumping over rocks in the fields. Then he took to jumping off the farmyard fence. After that he looked around for something bigger and better—and he spotted the hen-house roof. So he climbed up there and jumped off.

He liked the rush of wind on his face, the feeling of flying through the air, the plunk when his feet hit the ground.

Chickens flapped and cackled when he landed. Puffs of dust began to rise. Mrs. Patch came running to the rescue. She thought Sam was a heap of broken bones for sure, jumping off the hen-house roof.

"Look at this," she called to Mr. Patch. "Did you ever see such a child?"

Mr. Patch was mending the barn-door latch. He hadn't seen Sam leaping through the air from the hen-house roof. His nerves weren't all a-jangle, like Mrs. Patch's. He could calmly say, "Jumping's all right for a little boy. He'll settle down soon enough."

Did Sam settle down? Not so's you'd notice. He had long, springy legs, and he just couldn't resist jumping over things, and around things, and off things. He arrived for his first day of school by jumping over the schoolyard pump and then right on through the doorway. He nearly landed in his teacher's lap.

When the noon bell rang, he jumped from the top step of the schoolhouse and landed clear across the road, in Farmer Logan's corn field.

"Get on back to school!" Farmer Logan flapped his hat at Sam.

Sam jumped back across the road. His teacher was sitting on a bench by the schoolhouse, eating her lunch in a ladylike manner. Sam almost landed in her lap again. She could see things weren't going to be quite the same with Sam Patch in school.

The next day at noontime, all the other children began to follow Sam around. They tried to jump out of trees, and over the pump, and

down the schoolhouse steps. But they weren't born to jump, the way Sam was. Pretty soon the teacher was hearing a lot of wails and cries about skinned knees and sore ankles. Not to mention clothes torn on tree branches and ragged holes in the knees of trousers.

"This will never do," the teacher said. She closed school early and marched down the road to have a word with Sam's parents.

Mr. Patch was out in the field plowing, so he missed all the fuss. He didn't have to listen to the teacher's tales, so he could calmly say, "Jumping's all right for a growing boy. He'll settle down soon enough."

But by and by, even Mr. Patch began to wonder some. Sam wasn't a baby anymore. He wasn't a little boy anymore. He wasn't even a *growing* boy. He was a young man. He had lively brown eyes and a merry smile—and those long springy legs. And he was still jumping.

Sam got a job in the cotton mill in town. But he spent more time jumping over the machinery then he did working at it. Mr. Slater, who owned the cotton mill, tried to be patient. But it wasn't easy.

One specially hot summer afternoon as the mill was closing, Sam decided to jump off the mill roof into the river below.

"I'm just getting cooled off," he shouted as he zoomed down.

The mill workers were leaving for the day, and they stopped in the doorway to watch Sam.

Mr. Slater couldn't even get out the door to go home. Every doorway was cluttered up with people watching Sam.

Mr. Slater's patience was getting thin.

The last straw was when Sam started jumping into the river in the morning, on his way to work. All the people who worked in the mill lingered around the river bank to watch Sam jump. They were late to work one and all, and that was more than Mr. Slater could take.

"Sam, you're a nice young man," he said. "But you're messing up things around here. I don't think you're cut out to be a cotton spinner."

"No, sir!" Sam agreed. He gave Mr. Slater a cheery smile. "I'm a born jumper. That's what I do best and what I want to do most."

"Then you'd better go do it," Mr. Slater said. "You're not much help around here."

Everybody went back to work. Except Sam.

Sam had to go home and tell his parents he wasn't a cotton spinner anymore.

This time Mr. Patch wasn't quite so calm. But he started to say, "Jumping's all right for a young man. He'll settle down . . ."

Mrs. Patch had heard all this before.

"You've got to have a talk with Sam," she said. "He's got to learn to hold a job and make a living."

Mr. Patch could see the truth of that. "Sam," he said, "how would you like to be a sailor?"

"I'd rather be a jumper."

"You might like being a sailor," Mr. Patch said. "How about giving it a try? And you'd be earning pay again."

"All right," Sam said. "I'll give it a try. But some day I'll be a jumper and get pay for jumping."

Mr. Patch laughed. "Nobody gets pay for jumping, Sam."

18

"I will," Sam promised. "Some things can be done as well as others."

Sam-the-sailor was Sam-the-cotton-spinner all over again. He spent more time jumping off the boat than working on it. Every time the boat passed a bridge along the river, Sam jumped up onto the bridge and down off the bridge into the water. And just like the mill workers, the sailors stopped what they were doing to watch Sam. The captain was practically running the whole boat by himself. He could see there had to be some changes made.

"Sam," he said, "you're a nice young man. But you're messing up things around here. I don't think you're cut out to be a sailor."

"No, sir!" Sam agreed. "I'm a born jumper. That's what I do best and what I want to do most."

"Then you'd better go do it," the captain said. "You're not much help around here."

Sam didn't mind not being a sailor anymore. But he was wondering how he could tell his mother and father that once again he had lost a job—a job that paid money. He stood on the deck and tried to decide how he could tell them easy, so they wouldn't be too upset. But there didn't seem to be an easy way to do it.

19

While Sam was thinking, a flock of birds flew over the boat, and he looked up. There against the blue sky stood the mainmast, tall and straight—just inviting somebody to climb up and jump off.

Sam forgot about everything else. He scrambled up the rigging and stood at the top of the mast.

"Hey there, young man—better come down before you fall," someone called from the wharf. A curious crowd gathered as Sam stood high above the river on the mast.

"I'm going to jump!" he called to the crowd below. The people laughed and shook their heads. They thought he was just fooling.

But sure enough, Sam jumped. His highest jump yet. Straight down like an arrow from the tip of the mainmast into the river below.

As he swam over and pulled himself out of the water, the crowd began to cheer and throw money. Coins clinked and clattered on the wooden boards of the wharf.

It was Sam's first pay for jumping.

Some things can be done as well as others, and Sam Patch had proved it!

After that, Sam's career as a jumper sped along fast and fancy. He went up and down the rivers jumping from bridges, ship masts, and high buildings. Crowds always gathered, shouting, *"Hurrah, Sam!"* They threw money, and Sam spent that fast and fancy, too.

He bought himself a long-tailed coat and a high silk hat.

He bought a green satin vest and shoes with shiny buckles.

He bought a pet bear.

If you ever saw a startling sight, it was Sam Patch strolling through town in all his finery, leading his big brown bear on a gold chain.

Sam was having a grand time. He was doing what he did best and what he wanted to do most. And he was earning a living to boot! He jumped high and he lived high.

He stayed at the best inns.

He ate the best food.

He hired a manager to put notices around town and in the newspapers when he was going to jump.

Old Ben wouldn't have jumped off a peanut himself, but he was a great manager. The crowds got bigger and bigger. Everybody knew when Sam Patch was going to jump. And everybody came.

The money poured in faster and faster, and Sam's jumps got higher and higher. When he jumped 77 feet from the Passaic River Bridge in New Jersey, everybody said, "You can't beat that, Sam!"

But Sam kept right on looking for something bigger and better, just like when he was a little boy home on the farm. But this time it wasn't any dinky hen-house roof he spotted. It was Niagara Falls itself!

"Niagara Falls!" Old Ben's mouth fell open. "You can't jump off Niagara Falls, Sam!"

"Some things can be done as well as others, Ben. And Niagara Falls can be jumped off as well as any other place."

"But Sam, that's—that's—" Old Ben spread his arms and made a wild guess. "That's probably over 100 feet high!"

"Near about," Sam agreed.

"Sam, you're crazy! Why don't you just retire now? Passaic Bridge was high enough."

"First, Niagara Falls," Sam said. "Then I'll think about retiring."

There was a rocky spot of land called Goat Island at the top of the Falls, and Sam had a jumping-off platform built there. It wasn't a very big platform, and it was kind of rickety. But it was fine for Sam. He dressed it up with a flagpole and an American flag, and it was really something to admire then!

All the newspapers carried this notice:

I SHALL, LADIES AND GENTLEMEN,
ON SATURDAY NEXT, OCTOBER 17,
PRECISELY AT 3 O'CLOCK P.M.,
LEAP OFF THE FALLS OF NIAGARA.

On the great day, everybody came from miles around. They came on foot and on horseback, in clumsy farm wagons and grand coaches.

All the children came. Picnic lunches were packed. And everyone was arguing with everyone else.

They argued whether Sam would really jump from Niagara Falls.

And they argued whether he would live to tell the tale if he did.

People began gathering on the shores below the Falls in the early hours of the morning.

The whole crowd buzzed with excitement. Children ran around getting in the way. Folks gathered in bunches, still arguing.

By noon the sky began to cloud over.

"Rain's coming," the people said to one another. "Maybe Sam won't jump if it rains."

But a little rain couldn't stop Sam Patch. The first drops sprinkled his face as he climbed the platform over the roaring falls.

A hush fell over the crowd. The moment had come. Nobody had ever jumped from the top of Niagara Falls before in all the history of the world.

Sam stood on the platform a few minutes, bowing first this way and then the other, waving to the crowd on the banks below. He had on his "jumping clothes"—blue pantaloons, a white shirt, and a red sash. Sam always did things with style, and he was as patriotic looking as the flag itself.

The rain pattered down, but nobody in the crowd thought of leaving to take cover. They had waited all day for this moment.

At last Sam was through bowing and waving. He stood looking down into the water below. *Way* below. He smiled to himself as he remembered the jumps he had made when he was a boy. Farm fences. Schoolhouse steps. The hen-house roof at home. Now Niagara Falls. Sam Patch had come a long way up in the world.

The crowd held its breath as Sam plunged into the waters. Then the silence began to give way to murmurs. "Where is he?" "Do you see him?"

Then—Sam's head bobbed up—his wet hair plastered to his forehead, a wide grin on his face!

The crowd went wild. Such shouts and cheers and yells you never heard. The whole state of New York must have echoed with the sound. When Sam swam ashore, the crowd seized him up, dripping wet, and paraded through town carrying him on their shoulders.

The band played.
Children threw their hats in the air.
People laughed and waved.

It was a great day of celebration. Some things can be done as well as others, and Sam Patch had proved it again.

"I hope you're satisfied," Old Ben said to Sam when all the fuss was over. "You'll retire now, like you promised?"

Sam wasn't very happy about giving up jumping. But he had jumped from Niagara Falls. *Niagara Falls*. After *that* jump, it didn't seem very exciting to go back to bridges and rooftops and such tame things.

The October days were chilly and dreary. Leaves fluttered from the trees. Winter was coming. Sam traveled about a bit, making speeches, showing off his fine clothes and his pet bear. "What are you going to jump off next, Sam?" everybody wanted to know. Young boys and girls tugged at his coattails in the streets. People stuck their heads out of farmhouse windows. Shopkeepers came to their doors. Everybody wanted to know.

"Why, I jumped off Niagara Falls," Sam would say. "I'm retired now."

One dusky evening Sam and Old Ben were sitting beside the fireplace at an inn, drinking from frosty mugs. The pet bear was stretched before the hearth, peaceful as a pup. Firelight glittered on his gold collar and chain. The innkeeper was dozing in a corner by the window, where the sky was darkening to night.

Sam and Ben looked up as a gentleman in a gray traveling cloak came in and walked over to warm himself by the fire. "Aren't you Sam Patch, the jumper?" he asked.

"I am," Sam answered proudly. It wasn't hard to spot Sam Patch with his long legs and fancy clothes and pet bear.

"I hear you retired. Not jumping anymore."

"Sam jumped off Niagara Falls," Old Ben said. "Can't get any more daring than that."

"What if you could?" the man asked.

Old Ben just shook his head, but Sam looked interested. "What if you could?" the man asked again. "Would you be afraid to jump?"

"*Afraid!*" Sam laughed. "There's no jump in the world I'd be afraid of."

"I'm from Rochester in upstate New York," the man said. "Genesee Falls up there is a higher jump than Niagara."

"Is that a fact?"

Old Ben could see the gleam of interest in Sam's eyes, and he felt uneasy. He didn't like this strange man urging Sam on. Sam was retired.

"Genesee Falls is a higher jump than Niagara," the man repeated. "And the waters are wilder."

37

"Now hold on—" Old Ben started to say, but nobody was listening.

"Too high for you, Sam?" the stranger asked. "Here's my money to say it is." He threw a gold coin on the table. It rolled a bit and came to rest. The bear stirred and opened his dark eyes.

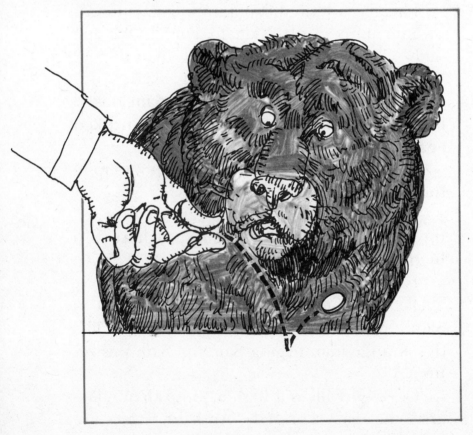

"And here's my money to say it isn't too high!" Sam threw down his own gold coin beside the other.

The man looked at the two gold coins in the firelight. "All right, Sam Patch. Set your day."

"Saturday," Sam declared without batting an eye.

"Now, Sam, hold on—stop and think—" Old Ben's words fell on deaf ears. Sam had accepted the dare to jump from Genesee Falls. His mind was made up.

"Just one more jump, Ben," he promised. "One last jump."

Sam wrote the newspaper notice with a flourish. And the excitement about his jump from Genesee Falls was even greater than the excitement about Niagara Falls.

HIGHER YET! SAM'S LAST JUMP! SOME THINGS CAN BE DONE AS WELL AS OTHERS.

People streamed to Genesee Falls and packed the shores. They started arriving before dawn and waited through the cold November morning. By afternoon the sky was dark. Thunder rumbled in the distance, and there were flashes of lightning beyond the hills. It wasn't going to be just a rainy day. It was going to be a stormy one.

"Can't you ever pick a sunny day?" Old Ben grumbled, to cover his worried feelings. "You're a darn fool, Sam Patch."

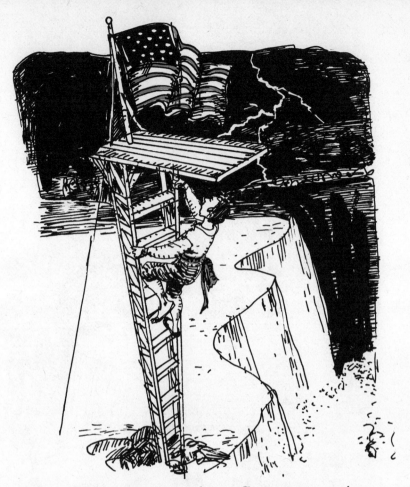

Once again the American flag was waving from Sam's jumping-off platform. It was a higher platform than the one at Niagara Falls. It towered into the air. And despite the growing storm, Sam climbed right on up.

"Don't jump, Sam! It's too dangerous! Come down!" the crowd called to him. But Sam stood calm and determined on his platform. The water below was a torrent of raging foam, dark as pitch under the black sky.

And then Sam jumped. At first there was a long moment of silence. Then the murmuring began. "Where is he?" "Do you see him?"

The voices grew louder and more frantic.

But no head bobbed up into sight this time. There was nothing to see but the rushing waters and the empty platform high above with the flag waving in the wind and rain.

The crowd became silent with fear. Sam should have appeared in the water by *now.* Everyone stared into the swirling river, searching for a glimpse of Sam. Little children drew close to their parents, whispering, "Where's Sam, Mama? Daddy, I can't see him."

Suddenly a shout went up from somewhere in the crowd. *"Get the boats, men!"*

And another shout. *"Find Sam!"*

Then everyone was shouting. *"The boats—the boats!"*

The men put out small boats into the stormy waters to look for Sam. They looked a long time. But they never did find him.

The leap under the thunderous sky at Genesee Falls was truly Sam's last jump.

Even so, people still talked about Sam Patch for a long time to come. Some of them believed he was still alive somewhere. Maybe he had floated on down the river. Rumors sprang up that he had been seen at Buffalo, at Niagara, and near the Pawtucket River in Rhode Island.

Other people said he had jumped so hard he went straight through to the other side of the world, and Sam was over there jumping and strutting and waving just like he always did.

But the truth was different. When winter passed and spring came, Sam's body was found at the mouth of the Genesee River.

After that, people said you could see his ghost at Genesee Falls on stormy nights. They said you could make him out when the lightning flashed, jumping from the great height above the Falls.

For Sam Patch was born to jump. It was what he did best and what he wanted to do most. And some things can be done as well as others.